TO: _____

FROM: _____

ISBN: 978-1-5460-3432-2

WorthyKids, Hachette Book Group, 1290 Avenue of the Americas, New York, NY 10104

Text copyright © 2021 by Jill Roman Lord
Art copyright © 2021 by Hachette Book Group, Inc.

Bible verse from New International Version, Scripture quotation marked NIV taken from the Holy Bible,
New International Version®, NIV®. Copyright © 1973, 1978, 1984, 2011 by Biblica, Inc.™ Used by permission of Zondervan.
All rights reserved worldwide. www.zondervan.com. The "NIV" and "New International Version" are trademarks
registered in the United States Patent and Trademark Office by Biblica, Inc.™

Library of Congress Cataloging-in-Publication Data
Names: Lord, Jill Roman, author. | Lakin, Brittany, illustrator. Title: Dream big, my precious one / written by Jill Roman Lord ;
illustrated by Brittany Lakin. Description: New York, NY : WorthyKids, [2021] | Audience: Ages 3–6. | Summary: "A narrator imagines all
of the incredible things a young child could become as an adult and inspires the child to passionately pursue dreams"— Provided by publisher.
Identifiers: LCCN 2020037077 | ISBN 9781546034322 (hardcover) Subjects: CYAC: Stories in rhyme. | Individuality—Fiction. |
Determination (Personality trait)—Fiction. | Self-esteem—Fiction. Classification: LCC PZ8.3.L877 Dre 2021 | DDC [E]—dc23
LC record available at https://lccn.loc.gov/2020037077

Designed by Christine Kettner

Printed and bound in China • APS
2 4 6 8 10 9 7 5 3 1

To Mom—thanks for always encouraging my crazy dreams. —J.R.L.

A big thanks to the folks at
Plum Pudding Illustration for being so helpful. —B.E.L

DREAM BIG, MY PRECIOUS ONE

BY JILL ROMAN LORD

ILLUSTRATED BY BRITTANY E. LAKIN

WORTHY® kids

I love to hold you close to me,
imagining all that you might be—
the things you'll do,
    the sights you'll see.

Dream big,
my precious one.

I think of all that you
might like—
will you climb mountains,
camp, and hike?

Perhaps play ball

or love to bike?

Dream big,
my precious one.

I wonder if you'll
play guitar,

sing lovely
like an opera star,

or kick a soccer
ball so far!

Dream big,
my precious one.

Perhaps you'll love to paint and draw;

build and hammer, nail and saw;

or dance so others
stand in awe.

Dream big,
my precious one.

You might become

a scientist,

a doctor

or zoologist,

a nurse

or archaeologist.

Dream big,
my precious one.

An astronaut exploring Mars,

an engineer designing cars,

a counselor to
help mend scars?

Dream big,
my precious one.

A preacher sharing
God's good news,

a captain on a
sailing cruise,

a vet to cure
sick kangaroos?

Dream big,
my precious one.

Or will you open your own store,

perhaps fight hunger, serve the poor,

or save the turtles
on the shore?

Dream big,
my precious one.

God gave you dreams before your birth
to work toward while you're on this earth.
He knows all you can do, your worth.

Dream big,
my precious one.

It won't just happen overnight.
You have to want it.
Work hard. Fight.
Train well and strive
with all your might.

Dream big,
my precious one.

You may fall short, but that's okay.
Then try again, a different way.
Keep trusting God, don't go astray.
Dream big, my precious one.

So work your hardest, mighty one.
Don't stop until you get it done!
You'll shine as brightly as the sun.

Dream big,
my precious one.

You see, your dreams aren't just for you.
They'll help out other people too,
change lives in ways you never knew.

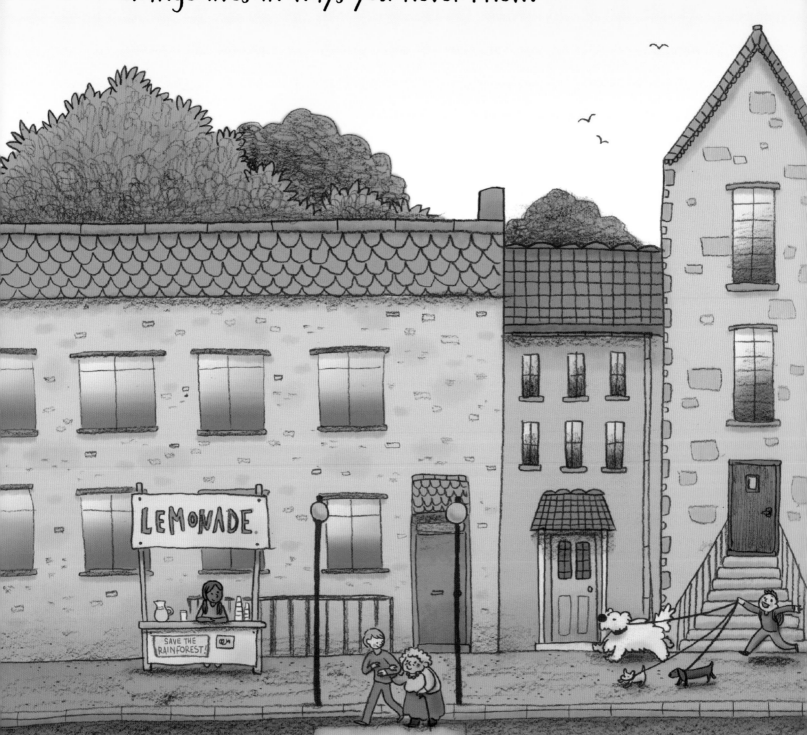

Dream big,
my precious one.

And when you reach your dreams and soar,
my precious child that I adore,
ask God to help you dream up more!

Dream big,
my precious one.

For now, I'll hold you close to me,
embracing all that you might be.
He'll take you far, just trust and see.

Dream big,
my precious one.

Be strong and courageous, and do the work.
Do not be afraid or discouraged, for the
LORD God, my God, is with you.
He will not fail you or forsake you.

—1 Chronicles 28:20